The Boxcar Children® Mysteries

The Pet Shop Mystery
The Mystery of the Secret Message
The Firehouse Mystery
The Mystery in San Francisco
The Niagara Falls Mystery
The Mystery at the Alamo
The Outer Space Mystery
The Soccer Mystery
The Mystery in the Old Attic
The Growling Bear Mystery
The Mystery of the Lake Monster
The Mystery at Peacock Hall
The Windy City Mystery
The Black Pearl Mystery
The Cereal Box Mystery
The Panther Mystery
The Mystery of the Queen's Jewels
The Mystery of the Stolen Sword
The Basketball Mystery
The Movie Star Mystery
The Mystery of the Black Raven
The Mystery of the Pirate's Map
The Ghost Town Mystery
The Mystery in the Mall
The Mystery in New York
The Gymnastics Mystery
The Poison Frog Mystery
The Mystery of the Empty Safe
The Home Run Mystery
The Great Bicycle Race Mystery

The Mystery of the Wild Ponies
The Mystery in the Computer Game
The Honeybee Mystery
The Mystery at the Crooked House
The Hockey Mystery
The Mystery of the Midnight Dog
The Mystery of the Screech Owl
The Summer Camp Mystery
The Copycat Mystery
The Haunted Clock Tower Mystery
The Mystery of the Tiger's Eye
The Disappearing Staircase Mystery
The Mystery on Blizzard Mountain
The Mystery of the Spider's Clue
The Candy Factory Mystery
The Mystery of the Mummy's Curse
The Mystery of the Star Ruby
The Stuffed Bear Mystery
The Mystery of Alligator Swamp

THE MYSTERY OF ALLIGATOR SWAMP

created by
GERTRUDE CHANDLER WARNER

Illustrated by Hodges Soileau

ALBERT WHITMAN & Company
Morton Grove, Illinois

Library of Congress Cataloging-in-Publication Data
is available from the Library of Congress.

The Mystery of Alligator Swamp
created by Gertrude Chandler Warner;
illustrated by Hodges Soileau.

ISBN 0-8075-5516-9(hardcover)
ISBN 0-8075-5517-7(paperback)

Cover art by David Cunningham.

For more information about Albert Whitman & Company,
visit our web site at www.albertwhitman.com.

Contents

CHAPTER	PAGE

CHAPTER 1

Welcome to the Bayou

"Look! An alligator!" Six-year-old Benny Alden rolled down the car window. He pointed toward a sheet of slick, dark water pierced by the stumps of trees at the side of the road. "An alligator," Benny repeated. He bounced on the seat. "I saw an alligator!"

"I think it was a big log floating in the water, Benny. Not an alligator," said his twelve-year-old sister, Jessie.

"Roll up the window, Benny," said his other sister, Violet. She was ten and the shyest of the four Aldens.

"Why? Do you think a big alligator might jump in?" Benny asked.

"Of course not," said Violet. Her expression said she didn't like that idea. "But it's so hot. Anyway, you've seen alligators before."

"Not in Louisiana," said Benny. "That was in Florida."

"Well, I don't imagine they're all that different here in Louisiana," Jessie said. "You know, big, lizard-shaped, lots of teeth."

"It's the state reptile of Louisiana," reported Grandfather Alden. He slowed the car down and peered ahead. They were on a narrow unpaved road. Trees draped in moss towered overhead and sheets of dark water stretched out beneath them.

"Why are we slowing down? Did you see another alligator?" Benny asked. He bounced even higher on the seat.

"Put your seat belt back on, Benny," said Henry. "Here, I'll help you."

Henry kept a close eye on his younger brother and his two sisters. Henry was fourteen, the oldest of the Aldens.

"No alligators," their grandfather said. "I'm looking for the sign. . . . There it is."

They all saw it then: a big sign, white with faded letters of purple and red that said, BILLIE'S BAYOU BAIT 'N BITE FISH CAMP & RESTAURANT. YOU'RE ALMOST THERE! Beneath it an arrow pointed the way.

They turned down a flat, wide, rutted road. Trees locked branches overhead, shutting out most of the sunlight. The air was very still and very hot. Benny rolled up his window, but he kept his face pressed to the glass, looking for alligators.

Jessie saw the Bait 'n Bite first. She pointed. "Through that gate," she said.

Grandfather turned in at the gate. As he drove across a tire-scuffed patch of sand, they saw that the Bait 'n Bite was perched almost in the water of the bayou beyond. Another low, small house with a long screened porch stood just past it, also right on the bayou. Tucked in the surrounding trees and not far from the restaurant on the other side along the bayou were small cabins, each with a small screened porch.

Opening the car doors, the Aldens tumbled out.

"Hey, there, James Alden," a voice called. A cheerful-looking woman with red curly hair springing out from beneath a purple cap was coming toward them.

"Hello there, Billie!" Grandfather called back.

"I was beginning to think you'd fallen into the bayou and were never going to make it to my birthday *fais do do*."

"What's a . . . a fay doe doe?" asked Benny.

"A dance. A party, *cher*," said Billie. "And *cher* means 'dear, darling.' It's what we call people. You're in the heart of Cajun country here — we Cajuns are the descendants of French Canadians who came to Louisiana almost three hundred years ago. So some of the words we use come from French. Some of our names, too, just like— "

Billie suddenly cupped her hand to her mouth and shouted, "Beau! *Beau!* Where are you? *Beau!*"

Everyone jumped.

"That grandson of mine. He keeps disappearing. Well, I'd know you anywhere, James. Your hair's a little grayer, I admit. But you haven't changed."

"You haven't changed, either, Billie Boudreau," Grandfather answered. His eyes twinkled. "I just hope you can swim better than the last time I fished you out of the bayou."

"I was twelve and I could swim fine then," she retorted. "I just wasn't going to let go of that new fishing pole."

They both laughed. Then Billie threw her arms around Grandfather Alden in a bear hug.

"Oof!" said Grandfather Alden. But he hugged her back, grinning.

Then he turned. "These are my grandchildren— "

"I've seen your pictures," Billie interrupted. "Let's see. This tall fellow is Henry. The little pepper here is Benny. Mmm, Jessie?"

Jessie nodded.

"And you must be Violet," said Billie. "Welcome!"

She threw out her arms and Violet took a step back. She was a little shy and she wasn't sure she wanted to have a Billie-style hug so soon after meeting her.

But Billie wasn't hugging anyone. She took a deep breath and shouted, "Beau!"

This time a voice answered, "I'm coming, I'm coming."

A tall, thin young man with wiry red-gold hair came around the side of the restaurant. Paint splashed his faded overalls and speckled his hands and arms.

"Now, where have you been all day, Beau?" Billie demanded.

"Uh, well, uh . . ." Beau's brown eyes shifted as if he were looking for an answer. "You see, uh . . ."

"This is Beau," said Billie. "My grandson. Staying with me for a while to help out. And to work on his art. He's an artist. Going to be famous someday."

Beau's cheeks reddened. "Ah, Gram Billie," he said. He ducked his head in a nod to the Aldens and added, "I'm glad to meet y'all."

"Well, grab a suitcase out of the trunk of the car," Billie told her grandson. She turned to Grandfather Alden. "I've given you the deluxe two-room fish camp with screened porch, right on the bayou," she said. "It'll be a snug fit, but I think you'll like it. Let's get you settled in."

A few minutes later, the Aldens found themselves standing on the porch of a small cabin about two hundred yards down the bayou from the restaurant. There was more porch than cabin, all of it screened in. "You can make up beds on the porch, looking out over the bayou there," said Billie. She motioned toward the water. "It's small, but it's not the smallest cabin in the camp. And it's private. You wouldn't know my shop was that close by, would you?"

"No," Violet almost whispered. From the porch, they could see only swamp and more swamp. It was as if the rest of the world had disappeared.

"It's not much bigger than our boxcar," said Henry. "I like it."

"Boxcar?" asked Billie.

"Yes. We used to live in a boxcar in the woods, before Grandfather found us," explained Jessie.

The Aldens told her all about the boxcar in the woods where they had lived when they were orphans and how they hadn't known their grandfather was looking for them.

"And that's when we found Watch," Benny said. "He lived in the boxcar with us, too."

"Then when Grandfather found us, he moved the boxcar into the backyard of our house and we can visit it anytime we want," concluded Jessie.

"Wow. What a story," said Billie. "Amazing."

"Yes," said Benny. "We have lots of good stories. We solve mysteries, too."

"Mysteries?" Beau spoke up at last. "What kinds of mysteries?"

"All kinds," Violet said. "We like to help people."

"And catch bad guys," said Benny. "We've caught lots and lots of bad guys."

"It's hard to keep a secret around my grandchildren," Grandfather said, smiling.

"Oh," said Beau. "Well. I have to go. See you later." With that, he practically bounded off the porch and out of sight.

The Aldens stared after him in surprise. Billie shook her head. "Honestly, I don't know what's gotten into that grandson of mine these days. Here one minute, gone the next."

They stood silently for a moment, watching as a small boat with two fishermen in it puttered by. Billie waved and the men waved back.

"Are they staying at the fish camp?" asked Jessie.

"No. Just neighbors. They live farther over in the swamp. More people live around here than you might think. We travel by water a lot. Some people can only get to their houses by boat."

The boat puttered out of sight. Billie said, "Well, come over to the Bait 'n Bite when you're ready. You're probably hungry."

"I'm always hungry," said Benny. Then he frowned and said, "You're not going to feed us bait, are you?"

"Nope. We use that to catch the fish. We use the fish to catch the customers! Or if you don't like fish, well, we could feed you gator."

"Gator? Alligator?" Violet gasped.

"Sure," said Billie.

"I don't think I want to eat any alligator," said Jessie. She wasn't sure if Billie was teasing.

"Why not, *cher*? Tastes like chicken." Billie laughed and pulled her hat down over her curls. Then she strode off toward the Bait 'n Bite.

CHAPTER 2

Ghosts and Gumbo

"I don't think I want to eat any alligator, either," Benny said. He finished unpacking and pushed his suitcase under the narrow bed at one end of the porch. He and Henry were sleeping at one end and Jessie and Violet were at the other. Grandfather had the tiny bedroom inside the cabin.

Grandfather overheard Benny as he came out onto the porch. "You don't have to if you don't want to, Benny," he said.

"Good," said Benny.

The Aldens walked back to the restaurant. But they didn't go in right away. Billie was out on the dock, talking to a tanned man in a bright orange cap. He had short hair that looked as if it had been hairsprayed in place and he kept flashing his teeth in a big smile as he talked to Billie.

She wasn't answering. She just nodded as she tied a boat to the dock and picked up a cooler off the pier.

"Hi!" Benny called, waving. "We're here. Is it time for dinner?"

The man flashed his white teeth again. "Oh, are you serving dinner? I thought the restaurant was closed on Monday nights."

"It's a special party for my friends," said Billy.

"Who came for your birthday celebration," said the man. "Right?"

Billie smiled very slightly. "Now I'm wondering how you might have heard about that," she said.

"Who hasn't?" asked the man. "But Beau, your grandson, was telling me, as a matter of fact. Interesting young man, Beau. Talented. Of course, it doesn't matter how talented he is if he spends his whole life on this bayou. The world will never know what an amazing artist he is."

Billie gave the man a narrow-eyed look. She didn't say anything. Instead, she turned and handed the cooler to Jessie. "Here. You can carry this for me. Empty the ice and wash it out with that hose by the side of the house there."

"I can do that," said the man.

"No, no," said Billie. "We've got it covered."

She seemed to be trying to ignore the man. She hadn't even introduced him.

He didn't seem to notice. He turned to Grandfather and said, "Hi. I'm Travis. Travis Bush. I'm a big admirer of Billie's place here."

"James Alden," said Grandfather, shaking the man's hand. "You like to fish?"

Billie made a noise in her throat that sounded like *Humph*. She picked up a tackle box and fishing pole and said to Jessie,

"Come on." She and Jessie walked toward the house.

Benny, Violet, and Henry stayed behind. They wanted to find out more about Travis Bush.

Benny looked over at the boats and counted, "One, two, three, four, five boats. Wow — Billie's got a lot of boats!"

"She could run a lot more boats if she wanted to. Really make this a big operation," Travis said. "She's got the ideal place for it. A little fixing up, she could be making a lot more money with a real fishing and vacation resort."

"I like it here the way it is," said Henry. He wasn't quite sure he liked this smiling stranger.

The stranger glanced in Henry's direction. "Yes, but you're not a businessman, are you, son?" he asked.

"Is Billie looking for a partner?" Violet asked.

"No. But I'm hoping I can change her mind. Or persuade her to sell this place to me. I'd give her a very good price," Travis said. "It would make a nice birthday present. She could retire. Travel."

Grandfather laughed and shook his head. "Billie was born and raised on this bayou," he said. "She's not going anywhere."

The man smiled again. Benny frowned. He didn't like that man's smile, not one bit. "We'll see about that," the man said. He nodded and strode off.

"I don't like him," said Benny. "He smiles like an alligator that wants to eat you."

"I know how you feel, Benny," Henry said.

"If you keep standing around out there, you'll never get dinner," Billie shouted from the front porch of the Bait 'n Bite.

"Come on!" cried Benny, forgetting about Travis Bush. He led the way as fast as he could up the pier and across the front yard of the restaurant. He banged open the screen door and crossed a wide porch filled with tables and all kinds of chairs. None of them matched. Each table had a colorful vinyl tablecloth held down with salt and pepper shakers shaped like alligators. Bowls of sugar and big bottles of hot sauce stood next to the salt and pepper shakers.

The sun was beginning to go down and the heat wasn't quite so bad. But the Aldens were glad for the big fans that whirled overhead.

Billie disappeared through another screen door. A few minutes later she returned, carrying a big bowl with a cover on it and the handle of a ladle sticking out from beneath. Behind her came Beau, carrying another bowl filled with rice.

When Billie and Beau sat down, Benny asked, "What's in the big bowl?"

"Gumbo," said Billie. "My own special recipe."

"Gumbo?" asked Jessie.

"It's a sort of stew. Made with okra and tomatoes and onions, among other things." Billie paused and said, "I was going to make chicken gumbo, but I couldn't find any chicken in the refrigerator. I know I had some."

"If it isn't chicken gumbo, what kind

is it? Does it have alligator in it?" Violet asked.

"Not tonight," said Billie, grinning. "Shrimp, fish, crab. Seafood gumbo."

"Oh, good," said Benny, holding out his plate.

Soon they were all eating gumbo as fast as they could.

"I thought I'd be too hot to eat, but I'm not," said Violet.

"Hot? This is nothing," said Billie. "Heat, mosquitoes, alligators, we have it all down here in the Atchafalaya Basin."

Benny asked, "The Achoo-fly-what?"

"The Atchafalaya Basin," repeated Billie. "That's the official name of all this water and swamp along this part of Louisiana." Seeing Benny's expression, she added, "Don't worry. You can call where I live Alligator Swamp. That's the local name for it."

"Are there more alligators here than in the rest of the basin?" asked Violet.

"No. But we used to have a famous alligator named Gator Ann. She'd come right

up by the pier down here and just float along. I guess she knew she was safe here."

"Safe from what?" asked Henry.

"People," said Billie. "People hunt them. Sell the hides, the teeth, the jaws, eat the meat. But I don't allow any hunting of anything in my part of this swamp. No guns. Fishing, that's it."

"Don't forget birdwatching," a voice as dry as the rustle of leaves said from behind them.

No one had heard him come in, but there he was, a man not much bigger, it seemed, than an elf. He wore a wide straw hat over hair that was almost the same color, patched and faded khakis, and an even more faded but unpatched long-sleeved blue work shirt. A pair of binoculars hung around his neck.

Billie didn't seemed surprised at all by the man's sudden appearance. She said, "My old friend Gaston Doucet, meet my old friend James Alden and his grandchildren, Henry, Jessie, Violet, and Benny. Gaston lives just down the bayou. He's a librarian."

"Retired librarian," rasped Gaston. "Full-time birdwatcher." He tapped the binoculars that hung around his neck. "Am I still invited to dinner?"

"Pull up a chair," said Billie. "I was hoping you wouldn't forget the time, out there in the swamp watching birds with those fancy new binoculars of yours. Is Eve coming?"

Gaston shook his head. He sat down and began to fill his plate. He took off his hat, but he kept his binoculars around his neck.

"She's not with you?" Billie asked.

Gaston shook his head again. "Went off with Rose today."

"Eve is Gaston's niece," Billie explained. "Rose is a guide with one of the swamp tours around here."

Gaston seemed content to let Billie do most of the talking. She went on, "Eve's about your age, Jessie. She's a swamp expert, same as her uncle."

Gaston smiled a little at that. But he shook his head and said, "She was turning into a good birdwatcher, too. But now all she thinks about is that ghost alligator."

"Ghost alligator?" Benny cried. He looked around as if he expected the ghost of an alligator to come walking through the door.

"Yep. The ghost of Gator Ann," Billie said. "At least that's what people say."

"Ghosts. Huh." Gaston snorted.

"Gator Ann? The alligator who used to live right out there in the bayou?" Jessie asked.

"That's right," said Billie.

Grandfather said, "Looks like you four might have another mystery to solve."

"No mystery," said Gaston. "Just some fishermen who've been out in the sun too long."

"They see the ghost in the middle of the day?" Violet asked nervously.

"Early mornings and late afternoons, right around dark, mostly," Billie said. "A fisherman will fish all day long, but anyone any good at fishing will tell you the fish bite best at dawn and at dusk."

"How big was Gator Ann?" Benny asked, excited by the idea.

"She was a big old gator, bigger than any of you," said Gaston. "No one knows what happened to her. She probably just lived out her life and died of old age."

"Is her ghost big, too?" Henry asked.

"According to those sun-fried fishermen," said Gaston. He gave Billie a narrow-eyed look. "And you make it worse, telling 'em all about it."

Billie shrugged. She had a mischievous sparkle in her eye. "Makes 'em be more careful. *And* makes 'em return the boats on time . . . before sunset."

"Well, if it keeps away the foolish people who don't appreciate an amazing place like the basin, then good for the ghost alligator," said Gaston. "Maybe I do believe in it, at that." He pushed his chair back and stood up. "A fine dinner, and it was nice to meet you all."

"Aren't you going to eat dessert?" Benny cried.

"Don't like dessert," Gaston said. He nodded and glided out of the room into the darkening night as quietly as a ghost.

The children stared at one another.

Billie laughed. "Gaston doesn't talk much," she explained. "But Eve makes up for it."

"When will we meet Eve?" asked Jessie.

"Tomorrow," said Billie. "When you meet Swampwater Nelson."

"Who's that?" asked Henry.

"He's a guide. He and his assistant, Rose Delane, run tours and are swamp guides. Nobody knows these swamps better than Nelson. I've arranged for Swampwater to give you four kids a special tour of the swamp, first thing in the morning."

"That sounds great," cried Jessie.

"Oh, it will be," Billie said. "You never know what's going to happen on one of Nelson's special tours, but it's always fun."

"Maybe we'll see a ghost," said Benny.

"Maybe you will," said Billie. She sounded amused. The Aldens could tell Billie didn't really believe in a ghost alligator.

Of course, they didn't, either.

CHAPTER 3

A Haunted Fish Camp?

Benny sat up in his creaky bed on the sleeping porch of the cabin. He'd thought it would be very quiet out in the middle of a swamp. But he was wrong.

It was noisy. Tree frogs shrilled from the trees. Bigger frogs croaked like bass fiddles from the darkness. He heard strange calls that he hoped came from owls.

No matter how hard he tried to go to sleep, Benny kept hearing strange sounds that kept him awake.

And he was hot. Even the thin sheet he

was clutching felt as heavy and hot as a blanket. He didn't let it go, though. He wanted to hold on to it in case he had to yank it over his head.

What was that? Benny tried to see in the dark. He couldn't. Remembering his flashlight by the bed, he decided to turn it on.

Slowly and carefully, Benny picked up his flashlight. Was that something walking out in front of the cabin?

He clicked the flashlight on — and gasped. "Oh!" he cried, jumping up. His feet got tangled in the sheet. He fell and the whole small cabin seemed to shake.

"What is it?" It was Jessie, her voice sharp. She always woke up quickly.

"Wh-who's there?" Violet's voice was slower, sleepier.

The porch light clicked on. Henry stood there, his hair sticking up. Grandfather came out from the bedroom. "Is everything okay?" he asked.

"Look! Look!" Benny almost shouted. He waved his flashlight. The beam of it danced

across the screen and the sandy strip in front of the cabin.

"At what? A ghost?" asked Henry, lifting his eyebrows.

"No. It wasn't a ghost. It was a raccoon," Benny explained.

"A raccoon won't hurt you, Benny," said Jessie.

"I wasn't scared," said Benny indignantly. "Just surprised."

"Well, the raccoon was scared, I'd say. It's long gone. Good night, everybody," Grandfather said. He turned off the porch light and went back to his room.

Soon everybody had gone back to sleep — everybody except Benny. He closed his eyes and tried very hard to go to sleep, too.

Swish, swish, swish.

Benny's eyes flew open.

Something was in the bayou, not far away!

Swish, swish, swish.

How did an alligator sound when it was swimming in the water? If it was a ghost alligator, did it make the same sound?

Swish, swish, swish.

Then, suddenly, Benny heard a thump, a crash, and a huge splash.

Benny imagined an enormous ghost alligator jumping up out of the swamp. He screamed and turned his flashlight on.

"Benny, what is it?" This time Violet was wide awake.

The porch light clicked on. Benny looked around at the faces of his family. "I heard it!" he said. "The ghost of Gator Ann!"

Henry grabbed his flashlight and flung open the screen door. The beam shone across the narrow strip of dirt between the cabin and the bayou and across the water.

Violet and Jessie got their flashlights, too, and did the same. Benny pushed under Henry's arm with his own flashlight pointed toward the bayou.

Nothing moved. They saw flat black water, drifting strands of moss in the branches of dark trees.

"I don't see anything," Jessie said.

"No ghosts. No alligators. Nothing," said Violet, sounding very relieved.

"I heard it! It went 'swish, swish, swish,' like an alligator swimming," Benny insisted.

"Is that how an alligator sounds when it is swimming?" asked Grandfather, who had stayed on the porch in the doorway of the cabin.

"Maybe it was a branch brushing the water," said Violet. "Or you could have been dreaming."

"I was awake," insisted Benny. He squinted, trying hard to see the shape of a ghostly alligator disappearing into the swamp. But he couldn't see anything at all.

Violet yawned. "We have to get some sleep, Benny," she said.

"Okay," said Benny. "I guess it wasn't the ghost of Gator Ann."

"No," said Jessie. "Well, good night."

They all went back to bed. Benny lay down. But he held on to his flashlight, just in case.

"Wake up, Benny." Benny opened his eyes. Violet was bending down to shake him awake by the shoulder.

Benny sat up. He unwrapped his fingers from the flashlight. It was still dark.

"Did you hear something?" he whispered.

"No. It's time to get up," Violet answered.

Jessie came out onto the porch and snapped the porch light on. She was already dressed and ready to go. "It'll be dawn soon," she reported. "Hurry up, everybody."

Benny hurried. Even though it was very early in the morning, it was already hot. He put on shorts, a T-shirt, and sneakers.

They went out quietly, so they wouldn't wake up their grandfather. They followed the beam of their flashlights down the short trail to the fishing camp pier.

The night was fading fast. Now light was beginning to show over the tops of the trees to the east.

At the dock, Jessie stopped and pointed. "What's that?" she said in a low voice.

Benny peered out at the bayou. Something pale and ghostly was floating in the water! Benny's heart skipped a beat. Then he realized it wasn't a ghost, but a boat. The boat was floating upside down!

"Do you think that's Mr. Nelson's boat?" Violet said.

"I hope not," said Henry.

Just then they heard the puttering of a motor. A boat came around the bend in the bayou and pulled up to the dock. A large man with a thick black mustache and coal-black hair curling under a broad-brimmed hat sat at the wheel at the front of the boat, steering. Near the back, by the motor, sat a young woman with long, beautiful black hair pulled into a braid. In the middle of the boat was a girl about Jessie's age.

Written on the side of the boat was SWAMPWATER NELSON'S SWAMP TOURS. Near the front of the boat was the boat's name: *Swamp Flower*.

"Hello, there, Aldens," said the man.

"Are you Mr. Swampwater Nelson?" asked Jessie.

"In person. Call me Swampwater. And these are my assistants Rose, motor-mechanic and a swamp fox almost as smart as I am, and Eve, who has the sharpest eyes in Alligator Swamp."

"Hi," said Eve.

Rose said, "What happened to that pirogue?"

"Pirogue?" repeated Jessie in a puzzled voice.

"It's what we call boats here. They're special boats that float easily in shallow water," Rose said impatiently. "And they're hard to turn over. Have you kids been fooling around with it?"

"No!" said Benny indignantly.

"We just got here," Henry explained. "That's how we found it."

Swampwater steered his pirogue out to the middle of the bayou. "It's Billie's old pirogue," he said. "The one made out of a hollow cypress log. Not one of these new-fangled boats we just *call* pirogues, but a real one. *Cher*, she is going to be mad when she sees this. That old boat is her favorite."

"Let's get it back to the dock, then," said Rose.

As the Aldens watched, the three swamp guides turned Billie's boat over and towed it back to the dock. Rose began to tie it back to one of the pilings. She stopped. "Look," she said. "This rope's been cut!"

It was true.

"Someone did that on purpose, then," said Swampwater.

"And that's not all," said Eve. She pointed. "Look."

Along one edge of the pirogue a large, jagged chunk was missing.

Swampwater frowned. "What on earth is that?" he said.

"It looks like something bit the boat," Violet said.

"What would bite a boat?" asked Jessie.

"An alligator!" said Benny. He was very excited. "We heard it last night. It came swimming up the bayou and bit the rope and bit the boat!"

Everyone stared at Benny.

"What are you talking about?" asked Swampwater.

Benny told the guide what he'd heard in the night. "Swish, swish, swish," he said. "That's what it sounded like. An alligator swimming."

"That's crazy," said Swampwater.

"No, it's not," said Eve. She was sitting bolt upright in the boat, her hands to her cheeks. "It's not crazy at all."

"The boat got loose, or maybe, someone cut it loose for a joke, and it bumped into something," said Swampwater.

"If that's what happened, then what's this?" asked Rose. She leaned over and pried something out of the bite-shaped place on the pirogue. She held it up.

"That's an alligator tooth," said Swampwater slowly. "And from a big alligator, too. Well, I'll be swamped."

No one spoke for a long moment.

Then Eve said quietly, "Swish, swish, swish. That's the sound I heard right before I saw the ghost alligator in Crying Bayou."

CHAPTER 4

The Ghost Alligator

"Eve, there's no such thing as a ghost alligator," said Swampwater loudly. His voice echoed in the quiet dawn.

Again no one spoke. But Rose looked nervous.

Then Violet asked, "If it wasn't an alligator, what was it?"

"Someone mean as a swamp rat, thinking it's a funny joke," said Swampwater.

"Or maybe someone trying to scare Billie," suggested Henry.

"Scare Billie? Who would want to do that?" asked Eve, looking surprised.

"Travis Bush. He's staying at the camp. He wants to buy it from Billie, but she doesn't want to sell it to him," said Jessie.

"Him. Huh." Swampwater snorted. "I'd like to see him sneak around in the bayou in the middle of the night. If he tried to do something like this, he'd fall in. He can't walk without tripping over his feet."

"No one's trying to scare Billie," Rose said. "Maybe it *was* an alligator."

"A ghost alligator," said Eve stubbornly.

Rose gave her a sharp look. She shook her head slightly, then said, "Let's get started. Put on those life jackets and climb into the *Swamp Flower* one at a time."

Quickly the Aldens obeyed and Swampwater pointed the boat out into the bayou.

Henry looked at Eve. "Crying Bayou," he said. "Where's that? And why is it called Crying Bayou?"

"It's a long way from here," said Rose quickly.

Eve nodded. "It's called Crying Bayou because that's how the wind sounds when it blows through that part of the swamp," she told them. "At least, people say it's the wind. Of course, some think it's a long-lost fisherman, crying to get home."

"Do you think it was the ghost of Gator Ann you saw there?" asked Violet.

Before Eve could answer, Swampwater said, "Now, why would Gator Ann, ghost or no, go all the way to Crying Bayou? Alligators have strict rules about where they live. Females, especially, like to stay in their own home pond. And that pond was Billie's bayou."

"I don't think it was Gator Ann," Eve said. "She wasn't mean, the way this gator was. Red eyes and big teeth and ghostly. I left in a *big* hurry!"

"It chased you?" Benny cried.

"I don't know. I didn't look back. I just turned the motor up high and got out of there as fast as I could," said Eve.

"Will we see it today?" asked Violet, shivering a little.

"No," Swampwater said. "Because there is no ghost. What you'll see if you look up on the branch of that tree is a snake."

"A snake!" Violet shrieked. That made all of them jump a little. The pirogue rocked, but it didn't turn over.

Sure enough, a big snake was looped around the branch of a tree overhanging the water.

"Does it bite?" Benny asked.

"Yep. If you get close enough to let it," said Swampwater. "It's a water moccasin. A poisonous bite, so if you see one, give it plenty of room."

"Don't worry," said Henry.

Swampwater, Rose, and Eve took the Aldens up and down the watery roads of the swamp. They passed brown pelicans perched on the ends of docks by fishing shacks. Ducks flew from the water as they turned into quiet channels. A raccoon peered at them from the shadows, then slipped away. They saw buzzards circling overhead. That made Violet shudder.

Rose said, "Buzzards aren't so bad. Think

of them as the garbage collectors for the swamp."

"Ick," said Violet.

"Wow," said Benny.

Swampwater laughed and pulled the boat closer to the edge of one of the bayous.

"Do people get lost a lot in the swamp?" Benny asked.

Swampwater answered that. "All the time," he said. "That's why you need a good guide."

"Have you ever gotten lost?" Jessie asked Eve.

Eve shrugged again. "I know my way around. To you, it all looks the same, but to me, traveling in the swamp is like going up and down streets in a neighborhood."

"And if you stay in Alligator Swamp, you'll see channel markers and the little yellow arrows that Billie put up," added Rose. She smiled a little. "I think she got tired of having to look for lost fishermen. Some of those city folks can't even read a map!"

"Speaking of alligators, look to your right," Swampwater said softly.

At first they thought it was a log. Then

the children realized that the log had small, shiny, half-open eyes.

"Oh! He's watching us," said Violet.

"She," corrected Eve. "She lives in this bayou. We call her Mossy, because the pattern of her skin looks like the sun through the moss in the trees."

Mossy's half-open eyes glinted as the pirogue glided by. But she didn't move. Benny didn't know whether he was glad or sorry.

Swampwater said, "Now, that one's no ghost. Told you not to worry about seeing ghosts."

Just then a boat came out of a narrow channel so fast that it almost collided with the *Swamp Flower*.

"Hey, watch it!" called Rose.

Two men were in the boat. One of them had bright red hair and was flapping his cap like a flag. He almost fell in.

"Sit down!" Swampwater shouted.

The man half sat, half fell down in the pirogue. "The ghost," he said. "We saw the ghost alligator!"

"Oh, no," said Eve. "Oh, no."

"Where?" asked Benny. "Where?"

"Back there," said the man who'd been waving his cap. "It slid out of the shadows and came straight toward our boat."

"Hold on," said Swampwater. "Back where?"

"It was that way," the man in the cap said. He waved wildly. "Ed here saw it, too." The man's friend nodded.

"Of course, it didn't try to eat them," Eve said. She sounded as if she were trying to convince herself. "Where did you see it?"

Ed, who was bald and had a round, red face, seemed to get redder. "We don't know how far," he admitted. "We kind of lost our heads when we saw it swimming toward us. It was still pretty dark and we took off and we got kind of turned around."

"But it wasn't far from here," insisted the other man.

"I see you're in one of the boats from Billie's fish camp," Swampwater said.

Nodding and wiping his sweaty face with

a damp bandanna, the red-faced man said, "That's right. We left yesterday afternoon for an overnight fishing trip."

"Which was going fine until that ghost gator came at us and Ed got scared and got us lost," said his red-haired friend.

"You wanted me to stick around and be alligator bait? We're not lost now, are we?" said Ed.

"Then you don't know where you saw the ghost," Eve said. She sounded relieved.

"No. Not really, I guess," admitted Ed. "But not far from here."

Rose frowned. She glanced over at Swampwater, then said to the two fishermen, "Come on. We're headed back to the Bait 'n Bite camp ourselves. We'll show you the way."

Beau was on the dock as they pulled up. He reached down to grab the rope from the boat of the two fishermen. "Hey, there," he said. "Good trip?"

"If you like getting lost and getting chased by ghosts and alligators," said the red-haired fisherman, scrambling out of the boat so fast that he made it bounce up and down on the calm water of the bayou.

"Wow," said Beau. "You saw the ghost alligator?"

Interrupting each other, the fishermen told their story.

"Looks like you caught some fish, anyway," said Beau as he helped them take gear out of their boat.

"Welcome back!" It was Billie, striding down to the end of the pier to join them. "You're early," she said to the fishermen.

"They say they saw the ghost alligator," Beau told Billie matter-of-factly.

"We saw it, and that's why we're back early. In fact, we're going to cut our whole fishing trip here short," said the first fisherman.

"Now, calm down," said his friend.

"You want to go back out there and get eaten alive?" the fisherman replied.

"Eaten alive by an alligator? Maybe by a ghost alligator? Sounds terrible," a new voice said. Travis, his eyes hidden behind sunglasses, was standing at the foot of the dock.

"What?" Billie looked dismayed. "But you've reserved the cabin for a week."

"We want our money back and we want out of here," said the red-faced fisherman. "Next time I go on vacation, it's going to be someplace where your life isn't in danger!" He turned to Travis. "You were right. There's a ghost in the swamp."

Eve nodded knowingly. Rose looked uneasy.

It seemed everyone was beginning to believe in the ghost alligator!

CHAPTER 5

Scary Stories for Breakfast

Travis smiled. The sun glinted off his white teeth and his dark glasses. "It's been chewing on the boats, too," he said, pointing to the ragged edge of the old cypress pirogue.

"Don't be ridiculous," Billie snapped.

"Biting boats? That's it. I'm getting out of here," said one of the fishermen.

"Now, wait just a minute," Billie said. She followed the two fishermen up the pier and across the clearing toward their cabin.

"I guess that ghost is not so good for business," said Travis.

Beau looked up. "No," he agreed. "My grandmother doesn't need all this worry. She was a lot more upset than she showed when she saw the cypress pirogue this morning. This camp is too much for her by herself."

"That's what I keep telling her," Travis said.

His eyes met Beau's. They looked at each other for a long moment. Then Beau picked up the rest of the fishermen's gear and took it up to one of the cars in the parking lot by the restaurant. He set it down and disappeared around the side of the house.

"Nope, that ghost is not good for Billie's business at all," Travis said to no one in particular. He turned his dark glasses toward Swampwater. "On the other hand, it might be very good for the swamp tour business. Ghost alligator tours — the tourists should love it." Travis smiled his alligator smile and strolled back up toward the restaurant.

Eve scrambled out of the pirogue. "I've got to go," she said.

"Wait!" said Rose. "Eve — "

But Eve wasn't listening. She almost ran up the pier, zipping past Travis and into the restaurant.

"I guess the ghost alligator really scared her," said Jessie as she climbed out of the *Swamp Flower*, too. Her brothers and sister followed her.

"It made Travis pretty happy, though," said Henry.

Swampwater said thoughtfully, "I don't like that Travis, now, but it's interesting what he said. The tourists have always liked it when I told them ghost stories from around the swamp."

Rose sighed. She said, "Nelson, it's almost time for our next tour. We have to hurry if we're going to make it back to the tour dock in time. And I'm on a tight schedule. Don't forget, I have the afternoon off."

Swampwater nodded. "Eve can walk back to join us, if she wants," he decided.

"We enjoyed the tour," said Violet.

"It was great!" cried Benny.

"Glad you enjoyed it," Swampwater said with a grin and a tip of his hat. With that, the *Swamp Flower* puttered away and Swampwater Nelson and Rose disappeared from sight around a bend in the bayou.

"Let's go find Eve," suggested Henry. "She knows all about the swamp. And I'd like to ask her a few more questions about the ghost alligator and Crying Bayou."

But when they got up to the restaurant, Eve was nowhere to be found.

"Well, if we can't find Eve, let's find some breakfast," said Jessie. "I'm hungry."

"I don't think Billie makes breakfast at the restaurant," said Violet.

"There's Grandfather!" Benny waved both arms. "Hi. We're back! We saw a ghost!"

"Ghost?" said Grandfather. "I didn't know you could see ghosts during the day."

"Oh, Benny, we didn't see a ghost," Violet said. "We met some fishermen who said they'd seen a ghost."

"But now we know there *is* a ghost," Benny argued. "The fishermen saw it. And we saw the bite it took out of the pirogue over there." He pointed.

Grandfather looked at the bite mark. "It sure looks like a bite. But when I was up here earlier for coffee with Billie, she was sure it wasn't," he said. "She said it was some person's idea of a joke."

"It's a ghost alligator bite," said Benny.

Grandfather said, "Well, whether it is or isn't, let's go get a bite of breakfast in town and you can tell me all about it. I told Billie I'd drive to the store and pick up a few supplies for her."

"Oh, good," said Benny.

Soon the Aldens were sitting down in a tiny diner in the nearest town. It was a small town, much smaller than Greenfield. They ordered breakfast and discussed the mystery of the ghost alligator.

"So three people that we know have seen the ghost," concluded Jessie. "Eve and those two fishermen. And Eve seems very frightened by it."

"Seeing the alligator made the fishermen

scared, too," Benny pointed out. "They ran away."

"They did leave. And Billie lost business," said Violet.

"That made Travis happy," said Jessie. She remembered Travis's shiny alligator smile and wrinkled her nose.

Setting down their breakfast plates, the waitress said, "Billie? You're staying at Billie's fish camp? Now, isn't that funny? I just had two fishermen through here this morning who'd been staying there. They were telling everybody about this ghost alligator they'd seen."

"Did you believe them?" asked Jessie.

The waitress shook her head. "There have always been ghost stories about the swamp. Some people will believe anything. I know Gaston Doucet — he's a bird-watcher who lives here — talks about the ghost alligator often. Course, Gaston's glad of anything that might keep people out of the swamps. Says they scare off the birds."

"Gaston's talking about the ghost alligator?" asked Jessie.

"Can't blame him. After all, it scared that poor little niece of his. And then there's that other fellow who's staying at the Bait 'n Bite who's always telling those ghost alligator stories in here, too. Black hair, sunglasses, big smile. I finally asked him if he'd seen the gator. He just laughed."

"Travis," muttered Jessie.

"He'll tell anybody who'll listen. Might as well take an advertisement out in the local paper. 'Stay away from haunted fish camp. Beware of alligator.' Terrible for Billie's business."

With that, the waitress bustled away to take another order.

"If business gets bad enough, Billie might be forced to sell the camp to Travis," said Henry.

"He's the one who told the fishermen about the ghost," Jessie said.

"And he's been spreading stories about it here in town," said Violet.

"Could he be the one who's behind all this? Turning over the boat, making it look like an alligator bit it? Somehow making it seem like there really is a ghost?" asked Henry.

"Swampwater said Travis would have fallen into the swamp if he tried something like that," Violet reminded them. "How could he do any of this?"

"And both Eve and the fishermen saw *something* out there," said Jessie.

"They saw the ghost. Because it's real," said Benny. "Besides, Travis was at the fish camp when we got back this morning. How could he have anything to do with those fishermen seeing a ghost?"

"Gaston knows all about the swamps, and he doesn't want more tourists around here," said Violet.

"Yes. He could have done it," agreed Henry.

"He and Billie seem to be awfully good friends," Grandfather pointed out. "Do you think he'd do something that would hurt Billie's business?"

"Maybe he doesn't mean for that to happen," said Henry.

"Then why turn over the boat at her

dock? Why not do it at someone else's dock?" asked Jessie. "Like at Swampwater's tour dock?"

"I don't know," said Henry. "Maybe we should visit Swampwater and take a look at his place. We could ask him some questions, too. We might learn something."

"I know another place we need to visit," said Jessie. "Crying Bayou."

"How would we get there?" asked Jessie.

"Borrow a boat from Billie," suggested Henry.

Grandfather said, "I think I'll come with you — I'd like to see more of the swamp myself."

"Okay," said Benny. "You can help us hunt for ghosts."

After they'd delivered Billie's supplies and gotten back to the cabin, Benny suddenly yawned. "I'm sleepy," he said in surprise.

"You got up before the sun," Grandfather said. "That's why. Maybe you need to take a nap."

"I could just lie down here on this bunk

and shut my eyes for a few minutes," Benny said.

He did. In only a few minutes he was sound asleep.

Grandfather said, "I'm going to sit in the shade and read until the hottest part of the day is over. Then we'll see about trying to find Crying Bayou."

"I'm not sleepy at all," Jessie declared.

"Me, neither," agreed Violet.

"We could go visit Swampwater's place," Henry suggested.

"Let's go ask Billie where it is," said Jessie instantly.

Grandfather had come out of the cabin with a book in his hand and overheard them. He took a chair over to the shade of the nearest tree and sat down. "Good luck," he said and began to read.

Violet, Jessie, and Henry went over to the Bait 'n Bite. It was very hot now. No breeze stirred the heavy gray moss that hung like long beards from the trees. Only the insects whirred and buzzed.

They found Billie in her bait shop in a

room next to the restaurant. An air conditioner roared in one of the two small windows of the room.

"Wow. It's nice and cold in here," said Jessie.

Billie looked up from a stack of mail she was sorting through and nodded. "I like to keep this room cold. My bait's fresh, but hot weather can make it smell pretty strong."

"Oh," said Jessie.

Unfolding a piece of paper from an envelope, Billie studied it. "Well, here's a mystery for you detectives."

"Mystery?" asked Violet.

"The mystery of the mysterious phone calls," said Billie. "This is the second bill I've had with a call to New Orleans listed for the Bait 'n Bite phone." She nodded toward a phone on the wall in the narrow hall that led into the restaurant. Above the old phone a faded sign read, LOCAL CALLS ONLY!!!

"You don't recognize the phone number?" asked Henry.

"Nope." Billie shook her head. "And I know I haven't been calling New Orleans." She smacked the bill down on a tray marked OUT on a shelf behind the counter. "Maybe I should get a pay phone. I hate to, though. Seems rude to my guests, somehow. Even if one of them is making phone calls they haven't paid for."

"Maybe the phone company made a mistake," said Jessie.

"Maybe," answered Billie. "I'll be asking about that, you can be sure. Now, what can I do for you three?"

"We wanted to visit Swampwater Nelson's tour place," Violet said.

"So you heard about his museum," said Billie.

"No. What museum?" asked Henry.

Billie grinned, running her hand through her red hair. "Well, it's more like a big sort of one-room cabin he built, full of things he's found in the swamp over the years. It's pretty interesting, I can tell you."

"It sounds as if it is," said Jessie. "How do we get there? Is it far?

"A good walk. Go out to the end of the road here and turn right. Walk until you see a sign on your right that says, SWAMPWATER NELSON'S TOURS AND SWAMP MUSEUM. Turn there and follow the road to his place. Can't miss it. It's dirt roads the whole way and hardly ever any cars. But stay on one side of the road, just in case."

"Thanks," said Jessie.

"And if you see any snakes, just give 'em plenty of room and leave 'em alone," Billie added.

"We will," promised Violet.

"And if you see that alligator ghost, you catch it for me before it gives me any more trouble!" Billie laughed heartily and ripped open another envelope.

The three Aldens exchanged glances. "We will," Henry promised. "When we find that ghost alligator, we'll take care of it, don't worry."

CHAPTER 6

Look and Listen

"Well, look who's here!" Swampwater was doing just what the three Aldens had left Grandfather doing — sitting in the shade of a tree, reading a book.

"Hi," said Jessie. "We came to see your museum."

"And to learn more about the swamp. And alligators," said Violet.

"You've come to the right place, my friends." Swampwater stood up and tucked his book under his arm. "Step this way to Swampwater's Swamp Museum."

They went inside the small two-room cabin. Like Billie's place, the cabin had a deep screened porch. It was right on the edge of the bayou, with a short pier over the water. Tied to the pier were two pirogues and a larger flat-bottom boat with bench seats and a canopy over the top of the seats for shade. All three boats had the words SWAMPWATER NELSON'S SWAMP TOURS on the sides, as did the house.

"Where's Rose?" Henry asked Swampwater. "Doesn't she help give the tours, too?"

"Ah, she's taking the afternoon off," said Swampwater. "Didn't say why, though. Maybe this ghost business is too much for her," he chuckled.

Jessie and Violet exchanged a questioning look. They'd hoped to talk to Rose a little more. Jessie remembered the worried look on Rose's face when Eve talked about the ghost alligator. Did Rose believe in the ghost, too?

Swampwater led the way across the small room from which he sold tickets for the tours, as well as sunglasses, hats, maps, and a few souvenirs. Swampwater put his book on a counter that, like Billie's, had an old-fashioned-looking cash register on it.

Jessie's eyes widened. "Look," she whispered to Violet. "His book. It's about ghosts!"

It was true. The book was called *Ghost Facts for Everyone*.

Swampwater opened a door on the one wall in the room where there wasn't a window.

A blast of cool air flooded the tour office. It was like diving into a pool, thought Violet, as she followed Swampwater and her sister and brother into the museum.

The Aldens found themselves in a larger room lined with shelves and glass cabinets. As at Billie's bait shop, an air conditioner roared noisily in one corner of the room. "Close the door behind you," Swampwater told Violet. "I keep it cool to protect my collection. The hot wet air in these swamps makes things get moldy and rot."

Violet quickly closed the door.

"Look at these!" Henry said.

"Alligator teeth," said Swampwater. "I find them from time to time."

"Alligator teeth," said Jessie, giving Swampwater a sharp look.

"And these are turtle shells," guessed Henry.

Swampwater nodded. "Found those, too. I don't kill things for my museum. Just take what I find in the swamp and give it a good home."

"What are these?" Jessie pointed to several curling, pale, leathery-looking scraps.

"Alligator eggs," said Swampwater.

In spite of herself, Jessie jumped back.

"Oh, they're not the actual eggs. Just the shells from an alligator nest, after the baby alligators had hatched. Believe me, I didn't try to get any eggs from a nest with the mother alligator sitting on it!" Swampwater said.

"Alligators build nests?" asked Henry.

"They do. They're ready to start having families when they're about seven or eight years old and about seven or eight feet long. The mother builds a nest, lays eggs, and

ALLIGATOR
EGG
SHELLS

takes care of the nest. She protects it and keeps it warm and even turns the eggs so they don't get too warm on one side and too cool on the other," Swampwater said. He pointed to a photograph on the wall. "There's a nest, with the mother next to it. Sometimes she sits on it. If you look closely, you can see the eggs."

Henry bent so close that his nose almost touched the picture-frame glass. "How big do alligators get?" he asked.

"Pretty big," said Swampwater. "I've seen fourteen-footers and I've heard of bigger."

"What do they eat? Do they eat people?" Violet asked.

"They're meat-eaters and they'll eat pretty much anything they catch — turtles, raccoons, dead animals. They'll even leap straight up out of the water to catch birds."

"And people?" asked Violet again.

Swampwater held up his hands. "If you swim in water where there is an alligator, an alligator might mistake you for something to eat. That's how most alligator attacks happen. And yes, I've heard of them coming after boats, too, when they think they're threatened by the boats getting too close."

"So you don't get too close to them, even in a boat," said Violet.

"That's right. They can be very dangerous, no doubt about it. You can't take chances with a gator," said Swampwater.

"The baby alligators are cute, though," said Jessie. She'd found another photograph on the museum wall. This one showed a mother alligator in the sun, surrounded by baby alligators. The young alligators had bright stripes and yellow blotches.

"Sometimes they stay around their nests for a few days. Then they take off. A mother alligator might just eat her young if they hang around too long," said Swampwater.

"Gross," said Violet.

"Hey, look! A *white* alligator," said Jessie.

They all turned to peer at a small stuffed alligator on the top shelf of a display case. It was a little over a foot long.

"Albino," said Swampwater. "Born without pigment. They don't live long in the wild. About eighty percent of all baby alligators turn into something else's dinner before they grow big enough to be safe. For an albino alligator, it's about one hundred percent that die very small, very young. I'm surprised this one lived as long as it did."

"Is anybody here?" demanded someone loudly from the office.

"In the museum," Swampwater called. "I'm coming."

He went back into the tour office. Jessie, Violet, and Henry followed. A group of people stood there, looking hopeful. "Is this the right place for a swamp tour?" a red-cheeked woman asked.

"It surely is," said Swampwater.

"Is the ghost on the tour? The one we heard about at the diner in town?" the man with her asked.

"Well, I can tell you about all kinds of ghosts," said Swampwater. "Step right this way to buy your ticket." Swampwater winked at the three Aldens.

"You should see the museum, too. It's great," said Jessie.

"Thank you for showing it to us," Violet said to Swampwater.

"Anytime, anytime," said Swampwater, as they left.

"A white alligator," said Jessie. "Like a ghost."

"Except no one's going to think a little tiny alligator like that is a big, people-eating ghost alligator," said Henry.

"And Swampwater says they never grow up. It's very sad," Violet said.

"It seems as if Swampwater might like the idea of a ghost alligator after all, though," said Jessie. "He's reading a book about it. And telling the tourists about it, too."

"It did seem that way," Henry agreed. "It seemed like it might be good for his tour business, unlike Billie's fishing camp."

"Do you think Swampwater could be the one behind it all?" asked Violet.

"I don't know," said Jessie. "But I think we do have to consider him a suspect."

"That wouldn't make Gaston very happy,

if lots of tourists came to see the ghost instead of being scared away by it," observed Violet.

Henry shook his head. "The more we know, the more mysterious this mystery gets."

"I know another suspect. What about Beau?" said Jessie suddenly. "Remember, Billie said he'd been acting awfully mysterious lately."

"And he thinks the camp is too much for Billie," said Violet.

"Maybe he and Travis are working together," said Jessie. "Maybe . . ." She stopped short. "Look," she whispered, pointing.

They'd almost reached Billie's camp. And there ahead of them, as if their talking about him had made him appear, stood Beau.

He wasn't alone. He was talking to someone.

"It's Travis," breathed Violet.

Quickly they slipped behind one of the big old trees at the edge of the road. Quietly they moved closer, keeping a sharp eye out for snakes.

"Well, I don't know," said Beau. "It's a good price, it's true."

"A better offer than anyone else will make you," Travis said. "And your grandmother will get used to it, trust me. After a while, she'll hardly even miss it."

"I'll have to think about it," Beau said.

"You've been thinking about it," Travis said impatiently. "Do we have a deal or don't we?"

"Just give me some more time," Beau said. "I need more time."

"Okay, but my offer isn't going to last forever," Travis warned. With that, he turned and walked back toward the fish camp.

Beau stood watching him go. Then he sighed. He looked around as if to make sure no one was watching. Then he pushed aside some bushes, stepped out past the children, and disappeared into shadows of the trees.

When they were sure he was gone, Jessie,

Violet, and Henry stood up. "Do you think Beau and Travis were talking about selling the fish camp?" Violet said.

"It sure sounds like it," Jessie said. "I can't believe it. Could Travis and Beau be working together to get Billie to give up the camp?"

"Look at this," Henry said. He pushed aside the branches where Beau had disappeared. Hidden behind them was a narrow trail leading into the swamp.

"Where do you think he was going?" asked Violet.

"I don't know, but he was sure acting mysterious about it," said Jessie.

"We could follow him," suggested Henry.

"We have to get back to the camp," said Jessie. "Besides, we should go when we know he isn't, well, wherever it is he's going on that trail. So he can't catch us."

"True," said Henry. "We want to catch *him*."

CHAPTER 7

Lost in the Swamp

Grandfather put on his life vest and looked up at Billie. She was standing on the dock. "I'd send Beau with you to act as a guide, if I could find him," Billie said.

"We'll be fine," Grandfather said. "Your map is a good one."

"Crying Bayou is a long way, though," Billie answered. "But the way is well marked. It's just outside Alligator Swamp. You'll see my signs right up to the edge of it. You shouldn't have any trouble."

When the Aldens had told Billie they

wanted to go to Crying Bayou, she had been surprised.

"We're going to see if we can catch that ghost alligator before it scares away more fishermen," Benny had explained.

"In Crying Bayou?" Billie had said.

"Where Eve said she saw it," Henry had said.

"Well, if that's where those fishermen think they saw it, too, they really *were* lost. It's a long way from here. As a matter of fact, I don't know what Eve was doing all the way over there," Billie had said.

Now she leaned over and set a cooler in the pirogue. "Something to drink if you get thirsty and some cheese sandwiches. Also peanut butter." She shook her head. "I'm out of chicken again, can you believe it?"

"Didn't we just bring you some this morning?" Grandfather asked, surprised.

"I thought so, but it's gone. I'm beginning to think I've got ghost chickens. They just get up and walk right out of my refrigerator." Billie shook her head. "Go on. We'll see you about sunset." She untied the rope that attached the pirogue to the pier and tossed it to Henry. "Good luck."

Jessie waved. Then she lowered her hand to her cap to shade her eyes even more. Who was sitting on the restaurant porch, peering out through the screen at them? She thought she caught a glimpse of dark glasses, but she wasn't sure.

Henry steered the pirogue around a bend and the camp disappeared from sight.

The afternoon light was different from the morning light, but the swamp looked much the same. Benny kept an eye out for alligators. Jessie and Violet read the map and Grandfather sat by the motor.

At a wide bend, another boat came into view. It was Swampwater, leading one of his tours. He and Eve waved.

The boat hummed onward, cutting through the dark, sluggish water. Birds swooped overhead and Benny spotted another snake looped through a tree branch. Henry was careful not to steer the boat under that branch.

"We've reached the end of Alligator

Swamp," Jessie announced, looking up from the map.

"How can you tell? It all looks the same," said Grandfather.

"Just ahead there is a short open stretch of water," said Jessie. "Straight across, we should see a white marker. It points the way to Crying Bayou. Not far up the channel, we'll see a tree with a split trunk. That's Crying Bayou."

A minute later, Henry steered the boat out onto a wide patch of water. They crossed it and Violet said, "There's an arrow." She pointed to a small white arrow made of wood, nailed to the stump of a tree.

Following the arrow, they turned up a very narrow channel. Branches leaned over the boat. "Watch out for snakes!" said Benny.

Luckily, they didn't see any. They passed the tree with the trunk split into three smaller trunks.

"We're here," said Grandfather.

He stopped the motor. The pirogue floated gently on the water.

They saw no sign of an alligator, living or ghost. Jessie said, "Do you think that's an alligator nest?" She motioned toward a big hump of mud and rotted plants and branches at one side of the bayou.

"With an alligator on it?" Violet asked, her eyes growing wide.

"I think it is an alligator nest, but an old one," Grandfather said. "No tracks in the mud, and no broken plants around it where something heavy walked through them."

"Let's look at it," Violet suggested.

Henry lifted an oar from the bottom of the boat and paddled enough to make the boat pull up next to the alligator nest.

"Make sure there are no snakes — or alligators," said Grandfather. "Use the paddle."

Henry gave the mound several good pokes with the paddle. Then he whacked the nest a couple of times. To everyone's relief, no alligators came roaring down the side of the nest.

"I'll take a look," Jessie volunteered.

"Me, too," said Benny. He jumped out of the boat after her.

It was a very big mound, almost like a small hill in all the flat water of the swamp. Keeping a sharp eye out for snakes or anything else that might bite, Jessie led the way up the mound. When she got to the top, she turned to give Benny a hand up.

They balanced carefully and looked down.

"Do you see anything?" called Violet.

"No," said Jessie. She studied the mound at her feet. "No," she said again. "It doesn't look as if anything has been here for a long, long time. At least, no alligators."

"No ghost alligators, either," added Benny. He was disappointed.

"No footprints? Alligator tracks?" asked Henry.

"No tracks," said Benny. He put his hands on his hips. "Ghosts don't make tracks." That was one of Benny's rules about ghosts. He didn't believe that ghosts left tracks.

"Any place where someone could have hidden and jumped out?"

Jessie laughed. "You mean, dressed in an alligator suit? No. No way that could have happened. It's a straight drop into grass and water behind me. No place to really hide."

She and Benny scrambled back down the alligator mound and into the boat. Henry turned it around. It wasn't easy in such a narrow channel. It took a long time. He didn't turn the motor on until they were facing back out the way they came. He was afraid of getting it stuck in the mud.

"I'm glad an alligator isn't chasing us," said Violet. "It would catch us for sure while we were trying to get the boat out of the bayou."

"No kidding. And you can't go much farther up this bayou. Look how narrow it gets just up ahead," Jessie said.

They headed back the way they came, across the short stretch of swamp pond. Violet and Benny each took a side of the boat and looked for channel markers and arrows. "There," said Benny, and Henry turned the boat.

"There," said Violet a few minutes later. "It's one of Billie's arrows," and Henry turned the boat in that direction.

They saw another arrow and turned again.

Suddenly Jessie said, "Wait!"

"What is it, Jessie?" asked Grandfather.

"This isn't right. We've made a wrong turn," said Jessie. She studied the map. "We've made lots of wrong turns."

"How could we? We were following the arrows," said Violet.

"I don't know," said Jessie. "But we're supposed to be headed west toward the fish camp, and we're not. We're going in the opposite direction. Look, the sun is setting behind us."

Sure enough, the sun was going down above the trees to the west — directly behind the direction in which the boat was headed.

"Let's take a look at that map," said Grandfather. He and Jessie both studied the map.

"We do appear to have gotten mixed up,

somehow," said Grandfather. "I think we need to go back the way we came."

But after they turned the first time, they couldn't find the next turn. Each channel looked the same. One tree was a lot like another.

"Maybe if we keep heading west, we'll find the way," said Violet in a small voice.

"We could do that," said Grandfather. "But maybe it would be best if we stayed where we are."

"That's what you're supposed to do as soon as you realize you're lost in the woods," Henry agreed. "It makes you easier to find."

"Lost," said Benny. "Are we lost?"

"Yes," said Jessie. "Yes, Benny. We're lost in the swamp."

"Lost," said Violet. Her heart sank. "Oh, no."

"It'll be all right, Violet. Billie can find us," Jessie said. She tried to make her voice calm. But she was worried.

Soon it would be dark. Then they would be lost in the swamp in the dark.

"It'll be night soon," said Violet.

"And we took lots of wrong turns," Benny said. "How will Billie find us?"

"And the swamp is so big," Violet almost whispered.

"Billie will find us," said Grandfather firmly.

Jessie said, "I don't know how we got lost. We followed the arrows."

"But didn't you say the arrows didn't match the map?" asked Henry.

"That's right. I didn't realize it right away. I was looking at the arrows and not at the map. I wonder if Billie made a mistake when she drew the map," said Jessie.

"Or maybe we just didn't read it right," said Violet.

"It's a pretty clear map," Jessie said. "Look."

"You're right. It's a good map. And the way to Crying Bayou isn't that hard — just long," said Henry.

Something swooped overhead and Violet squeaked.

"A bat, I think," said Grandfather. "Good."

"Good? Why?" asked Benny.

"Because bats eat mosquitoes. I hope that bat eats lots of mosquitoes before they all eat me," said Grandfather.

"Oh," said Benny.

Violet said, "Bats won't hurt you, Benny. Don't worry."

"I'm not worried!" declared Benny. "And maybe we'll see the alligator ghost now."

Violet shuddered. "Stop talking about ghosts, Benny, *please*," she begged.

"Shhh," said Jessie. "I heard something."

"The ghost," whispered Violet in a little voice.

"No," said Jessie. "Shhh!"

They all got very quiet. Insects whined around them. A sluggish, hot breeze rustled in the trees.

"I didn't hear any — Wait!" said Henry.

They all heard it this time. A voice was calling. They couldn't quite hear the words, but it was no ghost.

"Over here!" Benny jumped up and the

boat rocked. Violet grabbed her little brother and pulled him back to his seat.

"Let's shout together," said Grandfather. "One, two, three!"

On the count of three, they all shouted as loudly as they could. When they stopped, a voice came through the trees, "Hellooooo . . . helloooooo . . ."

Once again they all called, and once again someone returned the call. They shouted back and forth until, suddenly, they saw a light come around the bend of the bayou behind them.

It was Billie and Gaston. Gaston lowered his binoculars as their pirogue drew up to the Aldens.

"There you are," said Billie. "I was beginning to get worried."

"We knew you would find us," Benny said stoutly.

Billie shook her head. "Huh," she said. "*I* didn't know it. Thought I might get lost myself. As if I didn't have enough to worry about, someone has changed all my arrows and all the channel markers in this part of the swamp!"

"What?" exclaimed Henry.

"Why would someone do a thing like that?" gasped Violet.

Gaston snorted and made a face. "Tourists," he muttered. "Playing stupid tourist jokes."

"I don't know," said Billie. "But we can talk about this later. Let's get back before it gets too dark to see your hand in front of your face."

Benny immediately held up his hand. "It's not that dark yet!" he reported.

That made Billie laugh. "Not yet. Come on."

A floodlight was shining above the dock like a lighthouse lantern as the two boats motored up to the fish camp. "Looks like we have a welcome-back party," said Grandfather.

"It sure does," said Henry. "Beau and Eve . . ."

"And Travis?" said Violet in a low voice. "Why would Travis be waiting for us?"

"Well, well, well," said Travis. "I didn't think you could find them. But you did." Was he disappointed? He sounded as if he might be.

"Oh, I'm so glad you're back!" Eve said. "I was so worried. I didn't know you were going with them!" She flung her arms around her uncle.

He hugged her, then said gruffly, "What's this, *cher*? You didn't think I could get lost in Alligator Swamp, now, did you?"

"No," said Eve slowly. "But . . . well, I'm glad you're back."

Travis shoved his hands in his pockets. "See anything out there?"

"Like what?" asked Billie sharply.

Travis shrugged.

"How about a piece of pie and something to drink up at the restaurant?" Billie asked, turning her back on Travis.

"Okay," said Benny. "And we can eat our sandwiches, too."

"Now that all the excitement is over,

maybe I'll have a piece of pie at the restaurant myself. If that's okay, Billie," Travis said.

"Everyone's invited," said Billie. But she didn't sound pleased.

"Good. I want to hear all about your lost guests. Of course, with only me and the Aldens left here as guests at your camp right now, I guess it's not such a problem. Still, getting lost in the swamp is bad business," Travis said.

"Not if you're found," said Violet.

Only Travis laughed.

When they sat down at the long table in the restaurant, Travis pulled up a chair and joined them, just like that. Benny leaned over and whispered to Violet, "He's invited to have pie, but does he have to sit with us?"

"Shhh! We have to be polite," Violet whispered back.

"Oh, all right," said Benny. "But I don't know if I like him. I think he's glad we got lost."

CHAPTER 8

A Secret and a Thief

Just then, Beau came out with pie in one hand and a stack of plates in the other. He set the pie in the middle of the table and began cutting fat slices for everyone.

"Mmm," said Benny. "Peach pie."

"Beau made it," Billie said proudly.

"It was nothing, Gram," said Beau, blushing a little.

"He's making my birthday cake for my birthday party this weekend," Billie went on. "A surprise."

"The cake and a few other surprises," said Beau. He blushed harder.

The children couldn't help but think of the conversation they had heard between Beau and Travis that morning. Was that about one of the surprises he had planned for his grandmother's birthday?

"My grandson — he's an artist and a chef," said Billie. "This pie is a work of art just as much as any of your paintings on these walls." She motioned to them.

The Aldens looked around. "You painted all these paintings?" asked Violet.

"Most of them," said Beau.

Travis looked up at a large painting that had a wall to itself at one end of the room. It was a swamp scene and very beautiful. He looked from the painting to Beau and raised his eyebrows.

Beau looked away.

"They're wonderful," said Grandfather.

"Thank you," said Beau, blushing more. He cleared his throat, then said, "So how did y'all get lost, anyway?"

"We followed the map," said Jessie. "But

then the map didn't match the arrows, so we followed the arrows. And then suddenly we were lost."

"So then we stayed where we were," Henry said.

Beau nodded. "It's the right thing to do. Otherwise, you just get more lost — and harder to find."

"Having all the channel markers and arrows moved around didn't help," said Gaston.

"What?" asked Travis.

"What I said," Gaston retorted. "Someone had been playing with the swamp markers. It was enough to get anyone lost who didn't know their way around."

"I'll go out and fix it first thing tomorrow," Beau said.

"I'll help," Eve volunteered.

Gaston said, "I thought you were helping Swampwater, since Rose is going to be away."

"He won't mind if I help Beau tomorrow morning," Eve said. "Especially since I went on all the tours with him today."

Travis pushed his chair back. "It's been an exciting day here at the camp, I'll say that. Ghost alligators, lost camp guests, boats with bites taken out of them." He shook his head. "I hope I won't be too scared to sleep tonight."

"I don't think you need to worry about that," said Billie.

She didn't return Travis's smile. After a moment, he left.

"I don't like him!" Benny burst out.

"Shhh!" Jessie said.

"I don't think he cares if anybody likes him or not," said Beau. "All he cares about is getting what he wants."

"The fishing camp," said Henry.

"Right," said Beau. "Among other things." His gaze shifted until he was staring at the large painting at the end of the restaurant.

"Well, he's not going to get it," Billie said. "Ghost or no ghost. Let's not waste any more time thinking about that."

"Who do you think changed all the signs in the swamp?" Violet asked.

"Tourists," said Gaston.

"If tourists did that, wouldn't they get lost themselves?" asked Jessie.

Gaston turned to look at her. "You're right," he said, sounding surprised.

"So it had to have been someone who knows his or her way around the swamp," said Henry.

"Right again," said Gaston.

"Well, that could be anybody who lives around here," said Billie. "But it had to have been done today. Gaston and I were over there fishing yesterday afternoon and the signs were fine."

"Yep," said Gaston.

"And I had a couple of fishermen come in later this morning from that part of the swamp and they had no problem, so who-ever did it had to have done it between lunch and the time you got over there, James," Billie said to Grandfather Alden.

Under her breath, Eve said, "The ghost alligator."

"What?" said Jessie, startled.

Eve glanced at Billie as if she didn't want

her to overhear. "The ghost alligator," she said. "You were going to Crying Bayou to try and catch it, right? The ghost paid you back by turning all the signs around."

The next day, the Alden children walked down the road toward Swampwater's museum. But they weren't going to the museum. They were going to follow the path that Beau had sneaked down the day before, after his mysterious meeting with Travis. The children knew that Beau and Eve had gone to put all the signs and channel markers back where they belonged. That would take a long, long time.

"It couldn't have been Eve who turned all the signs around, because she was on that swamp tour with Swampwater. We passed her, remember?" Violet said.

"But she left right after we got back from our swamp tour yesterday morning," Jessie said. "She was in a big hurry, too."

"I wonder where she went. And I wonder if she got back in time to help Swampwater and Rose on their morning tours," said Henry.

"It sure sounds as if Beau and Travis are in this together," said Violet. "Especially after what we heard yesterday."

"It did sound as if Travis were trying to get Beau to agree to help him buy the restaurant from Billie," agreed Violet.

"I like Beau," Benny said, skipping ahead. "I don't like Travis."

"It is hard to believe Beau and Travis could be behind all this," admitted Violet with a sigh.

"It's almost as hard to believe that Gaston or Swampwater might be," said Henry.

"Wait a minute," said Jessie slowly. "What about Rose?"

"We almost forgot about Rose," said Henry. "Maybe because she hasn't been around since yesterday morning."

"She said she had the afternoon off," Benny said. "I remember."

"She did," said Henry. "Swampwater also said she wasn't around for the afternoon tour when we talked to him at the museum."

"Here," said Jessie. She stepped to one side of the road and pushed the bushes aside. Ahead lay a faint path leading into the shadows of the swamp. The path looked firm enough, but dark water surrounded it.

They stared for a moment. Then Henry said, "I'll go first. Jessie, you bring up the rear. Violet, Benny, you stay in the middle. Everybody watch out for snakes."

"And alligators," said Violet in a small voice.

"And ghosts!" Benny said happily.

They began to walk. They stopped talking. Henry broke off a stick and used it to test the trail ahead of them.

A turtle plopped off a nearby log into the water as they passed, making them all jump. But they didn't see any snakes, alligators, or ghosts.

Gradually the path grew wider and there was less water. More light seemed to shine through the branches above them.

Then suddenly they saw a little cabin

standing in a clearing in the middle of the swamp.

"Oh!" said Violet in surprise. Somehow this wasn't what she had expected to find at all.

Benny pushed past Henry and walked boldly into the clearing.

"Benny, wait," said Jessie. But Benny was already testing the front door of the cabin. It wasn't locked. He pushed it open and stepped inside.

"Wow!" he said.

His brother and sisters were right behind him. They all stopped to stare. Light streamed through skylights in the roof of the tiny cabin. Along one wall, a table made of a wide, thick board on two sawhorses held all kinds of paint and painting tools. Canvases were propped all around the other walls and under the table. A very large canvas covered with a cloth stood on an easel in the center of the floor.

"This must be Beau's art studio!" exclaimed Violet.

Walking forward, Jessie raised a corner

of the cloth that covered the painting. She smiled a little. "I think I've found one of the surprises Beau is planning to give Billie for her birthday," she said.

They crowded around to peer at the painting. It was beautiful. It showed someone fishing in an old pirogue in a bayou at the first light of dawn. Brighter than the sun was the hair of the person fishing.

"That's a painting of Billie in her boat," said Benny. "It looks just like her."

"It's amazing," said Henry. "Billie's going to love it."

Letting the cloth drop back over the painting, Jessie said, "Well, we've solved one little piece of the puzzle. But we still haven't solved the mystery."

"Let's go to Swampwater's museum and look for more clues," Benny said. He didn't really think they'd find more clues, but he wanted to see the museum.

"Okay," said Henry. "Maybe we can find out where Rose is. That might be a clue."

"Or it might just be her day off," said Jessie.

"Let's go," said Benny, tugging at Henry's sleeve.

At the museum, they found Swampwater — and Gaston. Gaston looked angry.

"Hi," said Jessie. "We brought Benny to see the museum. He didn't come yesterday because he was taking a nap."

"I wasn't taking a nap. I was just resting my eyes," Benny corrected her.

"Step right on in. I'll be with you in a moment," said Swampwater.

"No, no, don't let me keep you," said Gaston crossly.

"Why don't you join me, Gaston? It's cool in the museum. It would cool you off," said Swampwater.

"I don't want to be cooled off!" snapped Gaston. "I'm angry, and with good reason!"

"Why?" asked Benny.

"My binoculars. My brand-new binoculars — gone!" he almost shouted.

"You lost them?" asked Violet.

"I did not! They were stolen," he fumed. "Stolen!"

"How could they be stolen?" asked Swampwater. "You never take them off. Billie and I think you might sleep with them on."

He was teasing, but Gaston didn't think it was funny. He gave Swampwater a sour look and said, "I took them off and put them in their box last night, in the car. It was after we got back from finding the Aldens here. Then I went inside for pie."

"That's right, you weren't wearing them," said Henry. "I noticed."

"Were they still there last night after you had pie?" asked Jessie.

"I thought they were," said Gaston. "But it could have been just the empty box. That's what I found this morning when I went out to my garage — an empty box."

"So someone could have taken them last night at the restaurant or from your garage," said Jessie.

"Not my garage," said Gaston. "It was locked. The only way in is through the door that leads from my kitchen into the garage, or with a key to the garage door. And no one broke into my house or garage last night."

"Maybe someone borrowed them," said Swampwater. "Did you ask Eve?"

"Hah. Anybody with any sense knows I'm not going to lend those binoculars to *anybody*," Gaston said. "No, someone's a binocular thief. And just *wait* until I get my hands on whoever did it!"

He turned. "I'll walk with you down to your boat," said Swampwater. "You kids can go on into the museum if you like. I'll be right back."

The children were glad to go into the cool room that housed the museum. Benny went from exhibit to exhibit while they all talked about what they had just learned.

"Whoever stole those binoculars had to have been someone at Billie's camp," Jessie said. "If it happened last night, it had to have been at Billie's, right?"

"Someone staying at Billie's," said Benny. "Travis."

"He is the only other guest besides us," Violet said. "Plus, he left before anyone else did. It would have been easy for him to just reach into Gaston's car and take them."

Benny said, "That makes Travis a chicken thief and a binocular thief." He sounded pleased at the idea.

"What do you mean?" asked Henry.

"Someone's stealing chickens from Billie's restaurant. And someone took the binoculars. Two thieves and they are both Travis!" said Benny.

"Oh, Benny," said Violet. "We don't know that. It doesn't make sense. Why would Travis steal chickens?"

"To help make Billie go out of business," said Benny.

"I don't think a few missing chickens are going to put Billie out of business," Henry said. "But I'm willing to believe a sneaky fellow like that Travis could have taken Gaston's binoculars. But believing isn't proving. We don't have proof."

"No, we don't," said Jessie. "But it has to all fit together somehow. I know it does."

CHAPTER 9

An Alligator Trap

"Hi," said Violet. Swampwater had just come into the museum.

"Poor Gaston," he said in answer. "He just got those binoculars."

"Maybe they'll turn up," said Violet.

Swampwater shook his head.

"When is your next tour?" Jessie said, changing the subject.

"This afternoon," said Swampwater. "Gaston came to help me with the morning one, since Eve was out with Beau. But Eve should be back for the afternoon tour."

"Is Rose still gone?" Henry asked.

"She is. She took a couple of vacation days. Wanted to go over to the big city. I guess she misses it," he said.

"The big city?" asked Benny.

"New Orleans," said Swampwater. "She used to work at the zoo there, before she came here. It's where she learned so much about the animals that live in the swamp."

"New Orleans," repeated Jessie.

"I wish I could see a white alligator," said Benny, who wasn't very interested in Rose's old job in New Orleans. He was looking at the little stuffed albino alligator that Swampwater had on display.

"Lots of people do," said Swampwater. "But albinos don't last very long in the wild. Some people breed them in captivity, but it's not the same." He paused. "I've heard of some white alligators at the zoo that aren't albinos, though, now that you mention it. I've never seen them, but they're supposed to be very rare."

"Can they live in the wild?" asked Jessie.

"I don't know. Like I said, they're extremely rare. The zoo has all the ones anybody knows about, I think."

"But in the wild . . . there are none in the wild?" Jessie asked again.

"No. I imagine they'd get eaten pretty quick, just like the albinos," said Swampwater.

"I guess I'm getting kind of hungry for lunch," said Benny. "Not that I want to eat an alligator."

Swampwater laughed. "I guess they would taste like chicken, Benny. I don't know. I don't eat gator myself. I like my chicken to be a chicken, if you know what I mean. Just like the old alligators do."

"Alligators like chicken, too?" said Benny.

"Sure. Some fishermen use it for bait when they're trying to catch them," said Swampwater. "Course, I guess you could use anything to catch an alligator. They aren't picky. But chicken seems to work."

"Maybe it wasn't Travis who stole the chicken from Billie, then," said Benny. "Maybe it was the ghost alligator."

"Maybe it was," Swampwater said. He

laughed and shook his head. "Funny things do happen in the swamp."

Jessie said, "They sure do, and we have to go. Come on!"

"Why?" asked Benny. "Are you hungry, too?"

"Yes," said Jessie. " 'Bye, now." She hustled Violet, Benny, and Henry out of the museum.

"What's the big hurry?" asked Henry.

"I want to make a phone call," said Jessie.

"A phone call? To whom?" asked Violet.

"You'll see," said Jessie mysteriously, and no matter how many questions they asked her on the way back to the fishing camp, Jessie wouldn't tell them anything more.

Billie was down at the dock working on one of the boats when the Aldens got back.

Benny raised his arm to wave, but Jessie stopped him. "No," she said. "I don't want her to know we are here."

She slipped around the side of the building and into the bait shop. Going to the OUT tray behind the counter, she took it down and began to go through the papers.

"Benny," she said. "Watch out the window and make sure no one is coming."

"Okay," said Benny.

Jessie flipped the papers over until she came to one of the phone bills that Billie had been complaining about. She ran her finger down it. "There it is," she said triumphantly. "The phone number for the mystery call to New Orleans."

"New Orleans," said Henry. He wrinkled his forehead, then said, "Where Rose used to work. Do you think Rose made that phone call? Why wouldn't she call from her own house?"

"I don't know," said Jessie. "I don't even know if she made the call. But I think this phone number is a very important clue."

She wrote the phone number down, put the phone bill back in the OUT box, and went over to the phone.

Jessie dialed the number. "We'll have to pay Billie for this phone call," she said. "Later . . . Hello? Hi, who is this? It is?" She paused and listened for a moment.

Then Jessie asked, "Is this where the white alligators are?"

Violet, Henry, and Benny stared at Jessie.

She didn't seem to notice. She grabbed a pen and began to scribble notes on the back of an envelope from the wastepaper basket, asking questions and nodding, as if the person at the other end of the phone connection could see her. At last Jessie hung up.

"Jessie, what is going on?" demanded Henry.

"I'm not sure," said Jessie. "But someone has made phone calls from here to the zoo in New Orleans, directly to the department that takes care of reptiles — including the white alligators. The ones that aren't albinos. They're called . . ." She glanced down at her notes. "Leucistic alligators. Albino alligators have no pigment in their skin and pink or red eyes. These alligators have blue eyes and white skin with some blotches on it. A fisherman found them in a nest and brought them all in."

"But what does that have to do with . . ." Violet's eyes widened. "Do you think the ghost alligator is one of the blue-eyed alligators?"

"A leucistic alligator? I don't know," said Jessie. "It seems like they'd have just as much trouble staying alive in the swamp as albinos do. But maybe that's what happened. Maybe there's one out there and Rose knows about it and is hunting for it. It would be pretty valuable."

"But why doesn't she just tell people that's what it is, instead of pretending a ghost alligator is out there?" asked Henry.

"Because she wants to catch it first!" said Benny.

"It makes sense," said Violet. "She could be telling everybody it's a ghost to scare them away. She'd be able to get an alligator tooth from Swampwater's museum without any problem. Then she could have damaged that pirogue and put the tooth there."

"She knows her way around the swamp, too," said Benny. "She's a guide. She could mix up the signs and not get lost."

"Are we sure it is Rose?" asked Violet. "What about Travis?"

"He could be part of it, but I don't think so," said Jessie. "I think he's just using the rumors about the ghost alligator to make trouble for Billie."

"Did she take the binoculars?" asked Benny.

"I don't know," admitted Jessie. "But Rose did work in New Orleans at the zoo. She knows about alligators, especially the blue-eyed ones."

"She also just took some time off. She said she was going to New Orleans, but maybe she didn't. Maybe she's right here, hunting for the alligator," said Henry. "If that's true, she could have taken the binoculars, maybe to make it hard for Gaston to spot any white alligators."

"If Rose is behind the ghost alligator of Alligator Swamp, we need to catch her," said Jessie, "before it ruins Billie's business and she has to sell it."

"How?" asked Benny.

"I have an idea," Violet said softly.

"What?" asked Henry.

"Well . . ." began Violet, and then she told them.

When she'd finished, Henry laughed. "That's a good idea, Violet."

"But we have to do one thing first," said Jessie.

"What?" asked Benny.

"Henry and I, since we are the tallest and strongest, need to learn how to push a pirogue with a pole. Then we can go fishing to catch a ghost alligator!"

"We saw it! We saw it!" Benny stood and waved his arms. By now Violet knew what to do without even thinking about it. The moment Benny had started to stand up, she'd grabbed the back of his life jacket. She held on to keep him from falling out of the pirogue as Henry steered it up to the dock at Swampwater Nelson's.

Rose, a hammer in her hand, looked up and brushed a wisp of dark hair from her face. She was back early from her trip. "What?" she demanded. "What are you talking about?"

Swampwater let go of the board he'd been holding in place for Rose to nail into the dock. "What's all the excitement?" he asked.

"The ghost alligator," Henry said. "We were out fishing not all that far from Crying Bayou and there it was."

"It came out of the shadows. It had big, big teeth," said Benny. He held his hands wide apart. "Teeth this big. It tried to eat us!"

"No! Oh, no!" exclaimed Eve. She had just come out of the tour office holding two steaming cups. She stopped so abruptly that coffee sloshed over the cups' edges.

"I doubt that," said Rose coolly. Reaching up, she took both cups of coffee and handed one to Swampwater.

"You don't believe us?" Violet asked.

"I believe you saw something. Not an alligator with dinosaur-size teeth," Rose answered. "Hold the board down, please."

Swampwater held the board down and Rose finished nailing it in place with swift, sure strokes of the hammer. Behind them, Eve stood as if she, too, had been nailed to the dock.

"Crying Bayou?" she said finally, almost in a whisper. She looked frightened. "You saw the ghost there?"

Jessie and Violet exchanged glances. Each knew what the other was thinking. They felt bad about frightening Eve like that. But what else could they do?

"Not far from where we got lost the other day," Henry said.

"We didn't get lost this time," said Benny proudly. "We made our own trail markers with chalk on the tree trunks, just in case. But we didn't need them."

"Near Crying Bayou?" asked Rose. "Really? Hmmm." She seemed surprised.

Benny nodded. "That's right!" he said.

With one final bang of the hammer, Rose finished her work.

"Well," said Swampwater. "Now I won't

be tripping over that board anymore. Thanks, Rose."

"Glad to help," Rose said. She glanced at her watch. "Anything else?"

"Well, there is one more board that needs a nail," said Swampwater.

After glancing at her watch and then at the sky, Rose nodded. She followed Swampwater down the dock. "After that, I have to go," she said.

"It'll only take a minute," said Swampwater.

Eve said, "May I get a ride home with you, Rose? I don't want to walk!"

"Okay," said Rose.

"I'll get my stuff and put it in your pirogue," Eve said. "So I'll be ready." She turned, then seemed to remember the Aldens. She turned back. " 'Bye!" she said and ran into the tour guide shop.

"We have to go, too," said Henry. "We have to get back to Billie's camp. It's almost time for dinner."

"Wait until we tell Billie what we saw!" said Jessie.

Henry turned the pirogue and they put-tered back down the bayou toward the Bait 'n Bite.

As soon as they were out of sight of Swampwater's museum, though, Henry cranked the motor up to make the pirogue go as fast as it could.

"Shhh!" whispered Jessie. "Did you hear anything?"

"Nothing yet," Henry said.

They were quiet again.

The pirogue was hidden in a narrow channel off the main one leading to Crying Bayou. The children had pulled branches and brush across it so they couldn't be seen.

Suddenly, Jessie hissed, "There! Did you hear that?"

"A motor," said Benny.

"Get down," Henry ordered.

They all crouched low in the pirogue, peering through the branches.

Out in the bayou, a pirogue came into view. It sped past and up the bayou.

Quickly the Aldens pushed their own pirogue out into the channel. But they didn't start the motor. Instead, Jessie and Henry both picked up poles and began to push the pirogue along as fast and as quietly as they could.

They reached the end of the bayou and stopped, drifting into the deep afternoon shadows.

Voices came through the trees loud and clear.

"We should set some bait here," said Rose's voice.

"I have some more chicken pieces," someone answered.

"Eve!" breathed Violet in surprise.

"I can't believe Marshmallow got out again," Rose said. She sounded cross. "I was so sure that pen was escape-proof. I just hope we find her before she gets a bad case of sunburn."

"I wonder how she got all the way over to Crying Bayou," Eve said. The Aldens could see them now. Eve had a bucket by her on the pirogue seat. She was holding binoculars to her eyes, scanning the far edge of the bayou.

"See anything?" Rose asked.

"Nothing," Eve answered, lowering the binoculars.

The Aldens didn't have to say anything. They all recognized those binoculars — Gaston's!

"We've got to find her. It's one thing to tell people there's a ghost alligator in the swamp to keep them away from her. It's another for them to actually see her," said Rose. "Anyway, after we set out bait and traps, we'll go and work on the pen some more."

"And we can check our traps on the way back and let any other alligators we've caught go," Eve suggested.

"Good idea," said Rose.

As the two talked, Henry and Jessie had been pushing their pirogue closer and closer, slipping in and out among the tree roots of the bayou. Now, with one final push on the pole, Henry shot the pirogue out into the main channel and in front of the pirogue in which Rose and Eve sat.

"Oh!" cried Eve, jumping back and dropping a piece of chicken into the bayou.

"What are you doing here?" Rose demanded.

"Catching a ghost alligator," said Benny. "And you're it!"

"I don't know what you're talking about," said Rose.

"Yes, you do," said Jessie. "We're talking about Marshmallow. That's the name of your alligator, isn't it? We heard you talking about her and we know she's no ghost. She's a white alligator with blue eyes — like the ones in the zoo in New Orleans."

Rose scowled fiercely at the children without answering.

Eve's mouth dropped open. "H-how did you know?" she stammered.

"Why don't we go back to Billie's," said Henry. "We can talk about it there. And you can tell Billie what's been going on."

CHAPTER 10

An Alligator Birthday

"I don't believe it!" Billie cried. "A white alligator? A real one?" She shook her head in amazement.

The Aldens, Billie, Rose, and Eve were sitting on the restaurant porch. Billie had put a sign on the restaurant door saying, DINNER DELAYED. COME BACK LATER.

"But albino alligators can't live in the wild. They get eaten almost as soon as they're born," said Billie.

"Marshmallow's not an albino," Eve explained. "She's a . . . a leucistic alligator, like the ones in the zoo in New Orleans. They have blue eyes. But they can still die of sunburn. And get eaten because they aren't camouflaged like regular alligator babies."

"I found Marshmallow when she was just hatched," Rose explained. "Right by a nest. She was the only one. I don't know if the others got eaten or if she was the only white alligator. She was very small. I scooped her up in my fishing net and I fixed a shady, safe pen for her where nothing could catch and eat her, and then I raised her. She's over four years old now and big for her age, because I've fed her well."

"It's hard to keep a secret that long," Grandfather observed.

"I figured it out," Eve said. "I wondered what Rose was doing with all the fish she caught. I followed her one day when she went fishing and saw her take the fish to Marshmallow's pen and feed her."

"And then Marshmallow got away — we caught her again, but not before someone saw her. That's when Eve and I started telling stories about the ghost alligator,"

Rose said. "We wanted to keep people away from that part of the swamp."

"You took Gaston's binoculars," Benny said to Eve.

Eve nodded, then looked down. "I'm sorry I did that," she said. "I hope Uncle Gaston won't be too angry. But it was an emergency. Marshmallow had gotten out again and those two fishermen had seen her. We had to find her in a hurry, before someone else caught her."

"Or she died of sunburn," added Rose.

"It may have been Marshmallow that took a bite out of your pirogue," Eve said. "I'm sorry about that, Billie. That was another reason we wanted to catch her as soon as we could."

"The chicken — you used it as bait to set the trap," said Violet.

"The chicken from my restaurant?" Billie sat up in her chair on the restaurant porch.

"Just a couple of times," Eve said.

"The phone calls to New Orleans. Why did you call the zoo?" asked Jessie.

"How did you know?" asked Eve, startled.

"I couldn't figure out where those calls on my bills at the phone here came from," Billie said. She nodded at the Aldens. "That took real detective work."

"Thank you," said Jessie modestly. "But really, it just took a phone call. We called the number and it was the zoo."

"I called," confessed Eve. "The first time to ask about white alligators — that was right after I'd found out about Marshmallow but hadn't told Rose I knew yet. The second time was right after she got away. To find out the best way to catch her."

"Then we finally caught Marshmallow again. I thought we were safe," said Rose. She glanced over at the Aldens. "Until you guys came up this afternoon saying you'd seen the ghost alligator."

Henry nodded. "It was a trick. We couldn't let Billie's place lose any more business."

"Didn't you think about that?" Jessie asked. "Didn't you care?"

Rose blushed a little. "I know. I'm sorry. I just wanted to take care of Marshmallow."

"By feeding her and every alligator in the swamp my good chicken," said Billie, smiling a little. She didn't seem very upset. "A ghost alligator that's real. Named Marshmallow. Who would have thought it? And detectives to solve the mystery, on top of that." Billie's smile turned into a grin. "I couldn't ask for a better birthday present."

"Really? You're not mad?" asked Eve.

"How could I be? Nope, the only thing that'll make me mad is if you don't have fun at my birthday party this Saturday." Billie chuckled. "Catching the ghost alligator — now, that's a birthday gift of a story!"

Just then someone knocked on the door. Billie waved. "Gaston! Just in time for dinner. And a story. A good swamp tale, and guess what." Billie winked at the rest of them as Gaston came in the restaurant door. "We found your binoculars, too."

The porch of the Bait 'n Bite hummed with the noise of people eating and drinking, laughing and talking. Pirogues and ordinary boats lined the bayou out front. Cars filled the parking lot out back.

Rose and Swampwater Nelson came up to where the Aldens were sitting out on the pier. They were talking to Eve and peering, from a safe distance, into the very well-made alligator cage where Marshmallow was staying. It had mesh over the top and was locked. It was right by the pier and had a tarp over it to shield the white alligator from the sun. She was floating in it, looking as if she might be listening to what everyone was saying.

"Now that Billie has the ghost alligator where people can see her, business has been good," said Swampwater.

"Yep," said Eve. "I'll miss her."

"She'll be happier at the zoo in New Orleans with the other alligators," said Rose. "And now that she's bigger, she's too big for me to handle. But I'll miss her, too."

"How did anyone ever think she was a great big ghost?" Jessie wondered aloud.

"She's big," insisted Benny. "Much bigger than me."

"Well, I guess it depends on how you look at it," said Violet.

She knew that to Benny, Marshmallow looked huge. But to most people, she would have seemed small. She wasn't much more than four feet long. She had white skin with dark spots on it. Her blue eyes were startling to see, but she didn't look at all like an enormous ghost alligator.

"Pretty smart of you kids to solve the mystery," said Swampwater. "If you four ever need jobs in the swamp, you let me know. I believe you *might* be smart enough to learn the swamp guide business."

Benny cried, "A swamp guide! That's what I want to be!"

"Are you giving away my job?" said Gaston, coming down the dock to join them.

Swampwater grinned. "Nope. Not yet."

Looking from one to the other, Jessie said, "What job?"

"Swamp Tours for the Birds," said Eve proudly. "Uncle Gaston is going to be leading special tours for Swampwater. And I'm going to help. I'm even going to get binoculars of my own."

Her uncle raised one eyebrow. "Which you are going to pay for out of your tour guide assistant's salary," he reminded her.

They smiled at each other.

"Hey, y'all. Come on up here!" called Billie.

"Let's go," said Henry, laughing.

Everyone was still laughing when Beau banged on a table heaped with gifts near the front of the room. "Attention, everybody. We're going to have cake and Gram Billie is going to open her gifts — but this gift first."

With a flourish, he pulled a chair up to the giant painting at one end of the room and took it down. He turned and handed it solemnly to . . . Travis!

"My first art sale," said Beau.

Jessie poked Henry. "That's what he and Beau must have been talking about that day at the edge of the road. Travis wanted to buy the painting and Beau wasn't sure he wanted to sell it."

"I realized Billie wasn't going to sell me the fishing camp — at least not yet," said Travis. "But real estate isn't the only thing I'm interested in. When I saw Beau's painting, I knew I had to have it for my collection. This young man has a very promising career as an artist ahead of him."

"But . . . but wait a minute!" Billie was protesting. "I love that painting!"

Everyone else was applauding. They applauded even harder as Beau stepped down, tore the brown wrapping off a large square package, and stepped up onto the chair again. He carefully hung another painting in the place of the old one.

Billie's mouth dropped open. Cheers rang out.

It was the one that the Aldens had seen in Beau's studio — only now it was even more beautiful.

"Oh, oh, oh!" said Billie. "That's me! I can't believe it!"

She grabbed her grandson and gave him a great big kiss and a hug. Blushing, Beau said, "Awww . . ."

"Speech, speech!" cried Swampwater, and the cheering grew louder.

Billie jumped up onto the chair where Beau had stood. She raised her glass of root beer. "This has been some birthday," she said. "A beautiful work of art by my grand-son. Ghost alligators that are real. Old friends and new ones — who happen to be very fine detectives." Billie smiled over at the Aldens. "All I can say is, I hope every-one lives long enough to have such a won-derful, amazing birthday!"

Beau came out of the kitchen as Billie got down from the chair amid cheers and laughter. Everyone began to sing "Happy Birthday." The cake was ablaze with can-dles.

"Look!" said Benny. "Look! It's the ghost alligator! I mean, it's Marshmallow! Look!"

Benny was right. In the middle of the enormous birthday cake, surrounded by sugar roses and candles, was a white marzi-pan alligator with blue eyes — and a great big alligator smile.

GERTRUDE CHANDLER WARNER discovered when she was teaching that many readers who like an exciting story could find no books that were both easy and fun to read. She decided to try to meet this need, and her first book, *The Boxcar Children*, quickly proved she had succeeded.

Miss Warner drew on her own experiences to write the mystery. As a child she spent hours watching trains go by on the tracks opposite her family home. She often dreamed about what it would be like to set up housekeeping in a caboose or freight car — the situation the Alden children find themselves in.

When Miss Warner received requests for more adventures involving Henry, Jessie, Violet, and Benny Alden, she began additional stories. In each, she chose a special setting and introduced unusual or eccentric characters who liked the unpredictable.

While the mystery element is central to each of Miss Warner's books, she never thought of them as strictly juvenile mysteries. She liked to stress the Aldens' independence and resourcefulness and their solid New England devotion to using up and making do. The Aldens go about most of their adventures with as little adult supervision as possible — something else that delights young readers.

Miss Warner lived in Putnam, Connecticut, until her death in 1979. During her lifetime, she received hundreds of letters from girls and boys telling her how much they liked her books.